Dial Books for Young Readers

E. P. DUTTON, INC.      New York

# Noisy Nora

Story and pictures by Rosemary Wells

A Pied Piper Book
is a registered trademark of
Dial Books for Young Readers.
NOISY NORA
is published in a hardcover edition by
Dial Books for Young Readers
2 Park Avenue, New York, New York 10016.
ISBN 0-8037-6193-7
COBE
10 9 8 7 6 5 4 3 2

for Joan Read

Jack had dinner early,

Father played with Kate,

Jack needed burping,

So Nora had to wait.

First she banged the window,

Then she slammed the door,

Then she dropped her sister's marbles
on the kitchen floor.

"Quiet!" said her father.
"Hush!" said her mum.

"Nora!" said her sister,
"Why are you so dumb?"

Jack had gotten filthy,

Mother cooked with Kate,

Jack needed drying off,

So Nora had to wait.

First she knocked the lamp down,

Then she felled some chairs,

Then she took her brother's kite

And flew it down the stairs.

"Quiet!" said her father.
"Hush!" said her mum.

"Nora!" said her sister,
  "Why are you so dumb?"

Jack was getting sleepy,

Father read with Kate,

Jack needed singing to,

So Nora had to wait.

"I'm leaving!" shouted Nora,
"And I'm never coming back!"

And they didn't hear a sound
But a tralala from Jack.

Father stopped his reading.
Mother stopped her song.

"Mercy!" said her sister,
"Something's very wrong."

No Nora in the cellar.
No Nora in the tub.

No Nora in the mailbox
Or hiding in a shrub.

"She's left us!" moaned her mother

As they sifted through the trash.

"But I'm back again!" said Nora
With a monumental crash.